WHO IS
COMING
TO OUR
HOUSE?

WHO IS COMING TO OUR HOUSE?

By Joseph Slate
Pictures by Ashley Wolff

G. P. Putnam's Sons • New York

Library of Congress Cataloging-in-Publication Data
Slate, Joseph.   Who is coming to our house?
SUMMARY: The animals in the stable prepare for the arrival of baby Jesus.
1. Jesus Christ—Nativity—Juvenile fiction. [1. Animals—Fiction.
2. Jesus Christ—Nativity—Fiction. 3. Christmas—Fiction. 4. Stories in rhyme]
I. Wolff, Ashley, ill. II. Title. PZ8.3.S629Wh 1988 [E] 87-7319
ISBN 0-399-21537-9
7   9   10   8   6

To Lisa, Marilyn, and Toni
J.S.

For my own little boy
A.W.

"*Who is coming to our house?*"
"Someone, someone," says Mouse.

"Make room," says Pig.

"I will butt aside the rig."

"We must clean," says Lamb.

"Dust the beams," says Ram.

"Someone, someone," says Mouse.

"Sweep the earth," says Chick.

"Stack the hay," says Goose, "and quick!"

"Spin new webs," says Spider.

"I will line the crib with eider."

"Who is coming
to our house?"
"Someone, someone,"
says Mouse.

"Someone's coming from afar."

"I will nose the door ajar."

"But it is dark," says Cat.

"They will never come," says Rat.

"I will lay an egg," says Hen.

"I will spread my tail for them."

"Who is coming to our house?"
"Mary and Joseph," whispers Mouse.